The Story Puppy

Also by Holly Webb:

The Story Puppy

by Holly Webb
Illustrated by Sophy Williams

For Hattie

tiger tales

5 River Road, Suite 128, Wilton, CT 06897
Published in the United States 2021
Originally published in Great Britain 2020
by the Little Tiger Group
Text copyright © 2020 Holly Webb
Illustrations copyright © 2020 Sophy Williams
Author photograph © Charlotte Knee Photography
ISBN-13: 978-1-68010-483-7
ISBN-10: 1-68010-483-7
Printed in the USA
STP/4800/0385/1120
All rights reserved
10 9 8 7 6 5 4 3 2 1

For more insight and activities, visit us at www.tigertalesbooks.com

Contents

Chapter One
A Rough Day

Jack stared down at the page in front of him. The words seemed to be getting all blurry around the edges, and he blinked hard. He was not going to cry. He was not.

It wouldn't have been so bad if it were Mr. Gardner, their teacher, that he was trying to read with. But it was Mrs. Iqbal, Amarah's mom.

Jack had been really happy when Amarah told him that her mom was coming to help out with hearing their class read. He liked Amarah's mom— he'd known her for years, ever since Amarah's family had moved in next door.

It was different now that Amarah's mom was trying to get him to read out loud, though. Every time he saw her over the fence, he was going to remember sitting here. He'd been fighting to read this sentence for what felt like hours.

"Try and sound it out," Amarah's mom said gently.

"I can't," Jack muttered.

"I bet you can if you try."

"No, I can't!" Jack banged the book

down on the table. Rotten book! He'd thought it would be good when he picked it. He loved dogs, and the book had a photo of a glossy golden retriever on the front. The dog's dark eyes looked right at him and its tongue was hanging out, as though it had just been for a run.

It shouldn't be so hard—all Jack wanted to do was read about the dog. But the words just kept swimming away.

"Maybe we should take a break," Mrs. Iqbal suggested. "You've worked really hard today, Jack."

Jack didn't say anything. He fixed his eyes on the edge of the table, hoping the bell was going to ring. Waiting for Mr. Gardner to say it was someone else's turn to read. What made it worse was that he *had* worked really hard—he'd been trying and trying. But it was no good. The words just didn't make sense.

Mrs. Iqbal glanced around. "Oh— there's Evie. It's her turn to read next."

Jack was almost sure she was glad to get rid of him.

Jack slouched back down the hallway to his classroom. The rest of the class was doing math, and he was good at math. Numbers did what they were supposed to, not like letters. But he was still feeling miserable, and antsy, and upset. He didn't want to sit down and figure out fractions. Mr. Gardner would notice if he didn't get back soon, though, and their principal, Mrs. Bellamy, had a spooky habit of showing up whenever anyone wasn't in the right place.

Glumly, Jack opened the door to the fourth-grade classroom.

Mr. Gardner waved at him and said, "Amarah, can you show Jack where we're up to on the worksheet, please?"

Amarah nodded importantly, and as Jack slumped into the chair beside her, she started to point out the questions they'd been doing.

"All right," he muttered, grabbing a pencil.

"What's up with you?" Amarah asked, peering at him curiously.

"Nothing."

"Was it the reading?" Amarah sounded sympathetic, and Jack knew she was trying to be nice, but that didn't help. It wasn't fair! Why was it so much harder for him than for anybody else? And what if Amarah's mom told her that he hadn't been able to read? Then Amarah would think he wasn't smart. Jack's eyes started to sting again, and just in that minute, he felt so angry with Amarah. And her mom.

"My reading's fine," he snapped. "Leave me alone!"

"Don't be mean!" One of Amarah's other friends, Lily, pointed her pencil at him. "Amarah's only trying to be nice."

Jack glared at her. "Stay out of it, Lily. And stop waving that at me," he added, smacking the pencil out of her hand.

He had only meant to stop her

from wagging the pencil around—he thought it would just land on the table. Instead, it sailed across the room and hit Mr. Gardner's pants.

"Now look what you've done!" said Lily. She sounded half horrified and half excited. "You're going to get in trouble."

"Oh, no…," Amarah whispered, watching nervously as Mr. Gardner came over to their table.

"Since you all look guilty, I'm guessing this came from one of you?" Mr. Gardner said, sighing.

"I'm sorry, Mr. Gardner," Jack muttered, staring at the table. "It was an accident."

"No, it wasn't," Lily put in, and Amarah elbowed her.

"Be more careful, Jack. I'm watching this table." Mr. Gardner stood there for a moment longer, as though he wanted to say something else, but then the bell rang for lunch.

"What did you do that for?" Amarah whispered to Jack as she came to stand behind him in the line for lunch.

"Leave me alone!" Jack hissed back. And then when Amarah looked like she was going to keep on talking, he darted out of his place and went farther down the line to stand with Mason and James instead.

But all through lunch, he could feel Amarah watching him. She was sitting with Lily, like she usually did, but she kept glancing over at him, and she looked miserable. Really miserable and confused, as if she didn't know what she'd done wrong.

Jack didn't eat very much lunch.

The puppy flinched anxiously back among the weeds as another car roared past. She didn't understand what was happening. Were her people coming back? She'd tried to run after them when their car pulled away, but it was going much too fast, and she was limping. She'd landed awkwardly when they'd opened the car door and pushed her out—she hadn't expected it, and she'd banged hard against the pavement.

She lifted up her paw now and licked it, whining softly. She knew the way the car had gone, but she wasn't sure she could walk much farther, not with her leg like this. She'd have to wait for them to come back.

She hoped it would be soon. She was so hungry, and it felt like forever since she'd had anything to eat. The people had taken her mother away the day before, so she couldn't have milk, and they hadn't given her any dry food that morning, either.

The puppy had howled half the night with misery, and she still didn't know where her mother was. She was hungry and lonely and scared, and she didn't know what to do.

She huddled back again as the next car approached, but this time, the car slowed down as it passed her. It slowed down even more, and then stopped.

The puppy wagged her tail uncertainly. Had her people come back? Maybe her mother was in the car! She wagged a little harder and tried to sniff the air. She knew her mother's smell, but the scent was all mixed up with the dusty road and the sharp whiff of cars....

"Hey, sweetie … are you lost?"
Someone climbed out of the car and
began to walk toward her. The puppy
looked uncertainly up and down the
street. This was a stranger, she was
almost sure. Should she try to run? But
her paw…. She whimpered, and the
man approaching her slowed down and
began to talk again, his voice very soft.

"It's okay. Did you run away from
home? You're so skinny…. Don't be

scared...." He crouched down in front of her and held out his hand. "Where's your home?" he asked. "Come on, puppy, it's okay.... Come and see me...."

The gentle voice continued on, and the puppy wagged her tail again. She didn't know him, but he was slow and quiet, and he sounded kind. He might even have food, and she was so, so hungry.

Hopping on three paws, the puppy struggled over to the edge of the street and sniffed his outstretched fingers. When the man picked her up and snuggled her against his jacket, she just sighed and nuzzled in. He was warm and he smelled nice, and she didn't know what else to do.

Chapter Two
Figuring Things Out

Jack was in the yard, curled up at the top of the battered old slide, when he heard the back door bang.

"Are you up there?" his sister called. "Mom says do you want a banana?"

"Hate bananas," Jack growled. He didn't actually, but at the moment, he didn't feel like saying yes to anything. He'd gotten into trouble

for accidentally on purpose kicking
Mason's soccer ball too hard against
a window at recess, and he'd kept on
feeling sad and angry all afternoon.

"Okay." There was a creaking sound,
and Mattie pulled herself the wrong
way up the slide and came to sit next
to him. It was a tight fit with two, but
Jack was glad she hadn't gone away.
Mattie didn't say anything, just closed
her eyes and sat leaning back against
the wooden slats.

"Are you okay?" Jack asked. She
looked really tired.

"Got an essay to write." Mattie
sighed. She was a senior in high
school, and it seemed to Jack that she
always had a lot of work to do. Mattie
was always stressing about essays,

and she had to fit them in around weekend shifts at the supermarket and helping out at the animal rescue down the street. "I'm putting it off, but I've got to get it started before I go to the rescue. How about you?"

Jack didn't say anything. He hadn't told Mom about his awful day, although he thought she'd probably guessed something was wrong by the way he'd marched out of school glowering at everyone. Then he sighed. Mattie was easy to talk to. She didn't look worried like Mom, or start trying to think of a ton of ways to help. Mom was only being nice when she did that, but sometimes it made Jack feel worse.

"School was…." He stopped, trying to think how to put it.

"Not good?"

"Bad," he admitted, staring at his hands. "You know how Amarah's mom helps out sometimes?" He waved at Amarah's yard over the fence—it was beautiful, full of roses.

"With the reading?"

"Yeah. She was listening to me read—except I couldn't." Jack glanced sideways at Mattie. "The book was really difficult," he whispered. His voice was hoarse, as if he were about to cry. It was so hard saying it. "Difficult for me, I mean. Probably anyone else in my class could have read it."

Mattie slipped an arm around his shoulders. "I bet there are people in your class who aren't good at other things. You're really good at math."

"Even in math you have to read the questions," Jack muttered.

Mattie sighed. "I suppose so."

"It was horrible. I felt clueless, and I didn't know what to say. Amarah's mom was really nice about it, but I bet she thinks I'm not smart now. And what if she says something to Amarah?" Jack's voice shook.

"I don't think she'd do that," Mattie said comfortingly. "Hey, can I read with you sometimes? Mr. Gardner said it was mostly just practice you need. When he had that meeting with Mom about you getting help with your reading."

Jack leaned against her shoulder, feeling grateful. "That would be good," he agreed.

"Okay. Do you feel like doing it now?" Mattie peered sideways at him, doubtfully. "Or maybe when you're feeling better? We could do it before bedtime when I get back from the rescue."

"Yeah...." Jack nodded. He could see that Mattie wanted to help, but when was she going to find the time? She was so busy with her schoolwork and her job. And whenever she had a spare moment, she went to the animal rescue to help walk the dogs or sit and pet the cats. She'd told Jack that sometimes they needed reminding that people were nice. It seemed sad that the cats had to be shown that, but Jack had visited the rescue with Mattie, and he'd seen how hard the staff worked. They didn't have time to give the dogs and cats all the attention and love they needed.

Maybe I should ask Mom to help me with reading instead, Jack thought as Mattie shot down the slide and went inside to get going with her homework. Mom always offered, but usually Jack did everything he could to get out of it—saying he was tired, or he had math homework to do, or it was sunny so could he go outside and play with Amarah? He hated it when he got words wrong and Mom looked so worried. It made the words even harder to understand.

The puppy was hiding. This pen was more comfortable than the one she'd been kept in before—there was a soft bed and a clean water bowl and more food than she'd ever had. But it was different, and it smelled strange. It was noisy, too—there were so many other dogs here, all barking and howling and whining. Every time she settled down in the cozy bed, someone would start to bark, and she'd leap up shivering.

The puppy had nudged her bed toward the back of the pen, squishing

it up against the corner. It was big
enough that if she hopped over the
top and curled up tight, no one could
see her—or at least she hoped they
couldn't. The hard floor wasn't that
comfortable, but she felt better tucked
away.

The man who'd picked her up by the side of the road had brought her here. She'd huddled up on the car seat next to him, wrapped in his coat but still shivering. The car had growled and shuddered, and she'd hated it. What if he stopped and threw her out the door, just like her people had? When the car's engine finally died away and he reached over to pick her up, she'd cowered away from him with a whine.

The man had carried her into this place, whispering to her gently, but then he'd left her. He went away, and strangers had bandaged up her leg. It had hurt. They'd fed her and petted her and fussed over her, but she didn't understand what was happening. Were her people going to come back? Where was her mother? Why were all these other dogs here?

The puppy whimpered and wriggled her nose underneath the padded dog bed. It was dark there, and warm. She wriggled in farther, and she could almost not hear the barking.

Amarah grabbed the sleeve of Jack's sweater and pulled him ahead. Jack's mom was walking them all to school, but she was busy talking to Amarah's little sister Anika.

"What was wrong with you yesterday?" Amarah demanded once they'd gotten far enough in front. "Why were you being so mean?"

"I wasn't!" Jack protested, but he knew she was right.

"I had art club after school, or I'd have talked to you then. You can't just pretend nothing happened. You were lucky Mr. Gardner didn't send you out of the class."

Jack looked down at the pavement. "I know," he muttered eventually. "Thanks for trying to stop Lily from telling."

"You did hit her pencil across the room. You can't blame her."

32

Jack only nodded, and Amarah rolled her eyes at him. "So what made you so upset? It wasn't just Lily. You were angry before she said anything."

Jack's shoulders drooped, and he kicked the pavement with his toe. "It was your mom," he whispered at last. "Don't get mad!" he added quickly. "It wasn't her fault. She didn't do anything bad—she was listening to me read."

Amarah looked at him for a moment. Then she said, "I thought you liked my mom!" in a hurt voice.

"I do!" Jack said, almost in a wail. "But I couldn't read the book, and she must have thought I wasn't very smart. I was worried she would tell you."

"Oh…." Amarah looked thoughtful. "Well, she didn't. She said she'd had you for reading, but the only thing she told me about yesterday was that one of the girls in first grade almost threw up on her shoes."

"What?" Jack gasped.

"Uh-huh. Mom got her feet out of the way just in time. But when I asked who it was, she said it wouldn't be fair to tell me. She wouldn't say mean things about you, either, even if she thought them. And I bet she didn't." Amarah frowned, wrinkling her nose. "Actually, I just remembered something. She said she thought you'd had your hair cut and it looked nice."

"Oh…." Jack blinked. He'd been almost positive that Amarah's mom would tell her how terrible his reading was. He'd seen them talking about it so clearly in his head. It took him a little while to realize that he'd imagined the whole story.

Amarah nodded. Then she added, "What was wrong with the reading?"

Jack shrugged, but then he muttered, "Don't know. I just can't do it."

"Was Mom any help?"

"Ummm. Not really. I'm sorry." Jack glanced up at her anxiously. He really didn't want to upset Amarah again, but she just looked thoughtful.

"So … what are you going to do?"

"Practice with Mom. Mattie said she'd help, too, but I don't think she'll have time with all her school stuff and going to the rescue. And work. She's never home. I was almost asleep by the time she got back last night."

Jack sighed. "What else can I do?"

"I don't know." Amarah shook her head. "I'll think about it, though. There must be something."

"Maybe." But Jack looked doubtful.

Chapter Three
A Trip to the Rescue Center

Mattie slumped down on the couch next to Jack. "Want to do some reading now?" she asked, smothering a yawn. "I've got time."

Jack felt himself tensing up, but he nodded. "I'll get the book." He was still trying to work his way through the one with the golden retriever on the cover, but he wasn't enjoying it very much. It was too hard to get into the story, and he kept forgetting what had happened. He had read with Mattie and Mom a couple of times over the weekend, and he thought it might be helping, but it was all so difficult.

He and Mattie struggled through a page to the end of the chapter and looked at each other hopefully. "We could stop there," Jack suggested, and Mattie nodded.

"Mom's making dinner. It'll be ready in a minute."

"Did you go to the rescue after classes today?" Jack asked.

"Uh-huh."

"What's the matter?" Now that he looked at her closely, Mattie seemed really upset—Jack hadn't even noticed. His big sister tried not to tell him about the sad parts of working at the recue, but he knew she came home worrying about the cats and dogs a lot. Mattie rested her chin on her hands and heaved a sigh. "It's one of the new dogs," she explained. Then she looked at him. "You're sure you want me to tell you?"

"Yes…," Jack said, a little doubtfully.

"She's a puppy. Really little and so sweet. She's white and a little fluffy—

she probably has some Maltese in her, Susan thinks." Susan was the manager at the rescue. "I named her." Mattie smiled, but then her smile faded. "Her name is Daisy."

"Why are you sad if she's so sweet?" Jack asked, hugging himself tightly. He almost wished he hadn't let Mattie start telling him.

"Susan says she's not sure we'll ever be able to find a home for her."

"Why? What's wrong with her?" Jack frowned. Mattie was always telling him how the rescue workers were desperate to find good homes for all the animals. She really wanted them to adopt a dog, but Mom wasn't sure, with everyone in the family so busy with work and school. She didn't

think they'd be able to take care of a
dog very well. Jack thought they'd be
fine—every time he went to the rescue
with Mattie, he fell in love with a
different dog, but they hadn't managed
to persuade Mom yet.

"She's so nervous and miserable,"
Mattie explained. "She won't go to
anyone, and she hides whenever we
bring her food or we come to clean
out her pen. She doesn't trust people,
and she seems to hate being touched.
I think someone was horrible to her.
We get nervous dogs all the time—
and dogs who are upset because their
owners have died—and they hate being
in the rescue. But usually they start
to get a little friendlier after a while.
That's not happening with Daisy. She's

been at the rescue a week, and she still won't let any of us come near her. She's such a little dog—only a baby! It's not fair!"

"Oh…." Jack leaned against Mattie's shoulder. "That's really sad."

"I wish I could help her," Mattie said. "But I just don't know how."

Mattie was picking Jack up from school the next day—Amarah had art club, and Mom was working—so she took him with her to the rescue. Jack helped out, filling up food bowls in the kitchen, and then he went for a walk around. He knew all the staff and most of the volunteers by now, and no one minded him being there as long as he didn't upset any of the animals.

He tried to give some attention to a couple of cats, but they were dozing and only peered sleepily at him when he crouched down outside their pens. There was a whole litter of black-and-white kittens, though, who were more interesting. Jack watched them for a while, laughing as they stalked each other's tails across the pen and then collapsed and fell asleep in a furry bundle on the floor.

After that, he went to visit the dogs. He'd seen most of them before. There were a couple of elderly dogs whom nobody seemed to want to adopt—they'd been at the rescue for months. Jack's favorite was a wheezy, light brown pug. No one had been feeling very imaginative the day he was brought in, so he was just named Pug. He met Jack with excited squeaky barks, and Jack sat down on the floor

 by his pen and petted him through the wire.

Pug stood there with his eyes closed and his curled tail whirring while Jack scratched his ears and under his chin.

"Five more minutes, okay?" Mattie said, hurrying past. "Just got to help

Susan finish feeding everybody."

"Okay," said Jack, and then he had a thought. "Hey, Mattie!"

She turned around, walking backward with her arms full of food bowls. "What?"

"Which pen is the new puppy in?"

Mattie stopped. "Daisy?"

Jack nodded. "I just wanted to see her…," he said. He hadn't been able to stop thinking about the little white puppy, ever since Mattie had told him how unhappy she was.

"She's not any better, Jack. Susan told me. You'll just be upset seeing her."

"I don't care," Jack said stubbornly. "If you didn't want me knowing about her, why did you tell me?"

Mattie sighed. "I shouldn't have. Okay…. She's in the pen at the end. It's the quietest one. She doesn't seem to like the other dogs barking. I'm about to go and put her food bowl in, actually. You can come with me. Just … just don't scare her, all right?"

"Of course I won't!" Jack said indignantly. But then he nodded. "I promise I won't, Mattie. I only want to see her."

"You'll be lucky if you do," Mattie said over her shoulder as she went down the hallway. "When I went past earlier, she was hiding underneath her bed."

Jack petted Pug one last time and then got up to follow her. All the dogs knew it was time for their dinner, and they were watching excitedly as Mattie came along with the bowls. She slipped into the pens, talking lovingly to each of the dogs as she gave them their food. Mostly they tried to eat it before she had even put the bowl down. But when they got to the pen at the end, as far as Jack could see, it was empty. Then he remembered what Mattie had said about the puppy being under her bed. It did look lumpy in the middle. Was there really a puppy there, too scared to come out?

Mattie quietly opened the pen and put down the bowl. Then she came out again, looking worried. "We'll wait here for a minute," she said to Jack, beckoning him to come a little farther down the hallway, where they could just about see Daisy's pen. "I want to make sure she's okay. And check that she's actually eating her dinner."

Jack nodded and they both stood there, craning their necks sideways. After a minute or two, the dog bed shifted a little, and a whiskery white face appeared. Daisy looked around cautiously for a moment or two and then padded across the pen to her bowl. But she kept darting anxious glances at the hallway, as if she thought something scary was about to happen.

"She's so small!" Jack breathed in Mattie's ear.

"I know. She's probably about eight weeks old. That's just old enough to leave her mom. Isn't she sweet? She'd be adopted right away if she wasn't so timid."

Jack's stomach seemed to turn over inside him. Mattie had said that the puppy had been dumped by the side of the road. He couldn't imagine who would do that to such a tiny dog. Looking at her now, shivering as she tried to eat, he decided he'd do anything, anything to make her better.

Daisy was almost sure that someone was watching her eat. She could smell people—or thought she could. The smells here were all so strange and strong. The sharp scent of the spray the staff used to clean the pens seemed to sting her nose.

Whoever it was didn't come any

closer, though, so she kept scarfing down the food. The faster she ate, the faster she could hide herself away again. She didn't want anyone to notice her. It was safe there, tucked under her bed in the warm and the dark. It reminded her of being snuggled up with her mother. And even though the hard floor of the pen made her bruised paw hurt, it was definitely better being under the bed than in it.

She licked quickly around the bowl and darted away, burrowing back underneath the soft bed. Then she lay there, listening, tense all over, until she heard the footsteps going away.

Chapter Four
Something Amazing

Jack had only seen Daisy for a couple of minutes, but he couldn't stop thinking about her. She was tiny, and white all over, with soft ears and a stubby, scruffy little tail. Mattie said that breakfast and dinner were the only times they really saw her—two minutes of desperate gobbling, before she scurried back to hide under her bed.

"Susan and Adrian have both spent as much time with her as they can," she'd explained to Jack. Adrian was the other full-time staff member at the rescue. "Susan goes in and just sits in the pen for a long time. She's hoping that Daisy will get used to her being there and come out, although she hasn't so far. But they're so busy— the rescue is full again. Any time they spend coaxing Daisy to be friendly is time they have to take away from the other dogs and cats."

It didn't seem fair to Jack that Daisy needed help and everyone was too busy to give it to her. He wished *he* could help. But he wasn't old enough to be an official volunteer at the rescue. He didn't know anything about helping a dog like Daisy, either. He'd probably get it all wrong. But he definitely wanted to see her again—even if all he saw was a little hump under her bed.

So the next day, instead of going home with Amarah and her mom and Anika, he persuaded Mattie to come and pick him up. He told Amarah why on the way to school that morning— he didn't want her to think he was abandoning her. Once he had told her about Daisy, though, she was all for it.

"Can you take a picture of her?" she asked. "Mattie could take one on her phone, couldn't she?"

"Maybe while she's eating," Jack said. "Otherwise, it'll be a photo of a dog bed."

"That's so sad. I wish I could come with you. I want to go to the rescue anyway. Maybe we could persuade my mom and dad to get a cat."

"I could ask Mattie to take you with us one day," Jack suggested.

Amarah nodded. Then she looked at Jack, chewing her lip as though she wasn't sure what to say. "Did you finish that book?"

"Almost…," Jack muttered. Mr. Gardner had checked on their reading journals the day before, and he'd done his *I'm very disappointed* face when he realized Jack was still in the middle of the book about the golden retriever.

"Mr. Gardner said to do it last night!"

"Yeah, but I was at the rescue with Mattie." Jack shrugged. "I bet he didn't think I would anyway. He knows I'm terrible at reading."

Amarah eyed him doubtfully. "He sounded like he meant it to me. I hope you don't get in trouble again."

Jack looked worried for a moment, and then he grinned at Amarah. "I won't. We've got that history day, remember? There are people coming in to do a workshop. I'll finish the reading tonight. No problem."

"You'd better," Amarah said seriously. "I like our table the way it is—if you keep getting in trouble, we'll all be moved around again, and I'll end up sitting next to Lara or somebody else mean."

"All right, I will, I promise!" Jack sighed. "You're worse than Mr. Gardner."

"Do you want to help with getting the food ready again?" Mattie suggested.

"Definitely." Jack nodded. The more he did to help out, the more time Mattie and the others would have to spend with the animals. It was called socializing. Jack hadn't really gotten it when Mattie had explained it to him before, but now he saw how much love and attention Daisy needed.

He measured out the food for Mattie while she ferried the bowls to the pens. They'd finished getting all the dogs' dinners ready when Mattie suddenly stopped, frowning at him. "Hang on. I just remembered. Don't you have homework to do? Amarah said I had to make sure you finished your book."

"I can do it later!" Jack protested.

"Uh-uh. We'll go home, you'll have dinner, you'll be really tired—and you won't have time to finish it. Just go and sit in the visitors' room now."

Jack glared at her, but then he gave a huge, huffy sigh and went to get his backpack. Mattie was right, though. And so was Amarah—he didn't want Mr. Gardner moving them around in class, either.

He was searching through his backpack for the book when it struck him—he had to do the reading, but it didn't matter *where* he did it. Mattie had said that Susan went and sat in Daisy's pen to try and get her used to people. He couldn't do that—Susan would definitely say no, in case Daisy got really scared and nipped him—but he could sit just outside her pen, couldn't he? That would be almost as good. He could sit still and not scare her, and even though he had to sound out a lot of the words, he could do it quietly.

Jack hurried down the hallway to the pen at the end and sat down, leaning against the wall. The floor was a little hard, but it wasn't too bad. Besides, Daisy was lying on that hard floor all day.

"Hey, Daisy," he whispered. He could just about see the end of her tail sticking out from under the dog bed. "Are you okay? I've got to finish this reading homework, so I thought I'd do it with you." He looked at the bump under the bed for a moment—

almost as though he thought she might answer him. Then he shook his head and opened up the book, flipping through the pages to the right place. He was a *long* way from the end.

"Okay. So. Page forty-six. 'Benny … pushed the gate shut with his nose….'" Jack read on, slowly sounding out the hardest words.

He wasn't sure if Mr. Gardner would think reading to a dog counted as reading with an adult—especially since Daisy was only a puppy, and she wasn't actually listening—but Jack liked it more than reading to Mom or Mattie. He knew Daisy was there, so it still felt like he was reading to someone, but she didn't mind if he got the words wrong or took a while to figure them out.

Mattie fidgeted when he read to her. He was pretty sure she didn't know she was doing it, but she always fiddled with the hem of her sweater or jiggled her feet around like she was bored. Mom sat still, but she tried to help too much. She was always telling him not to worry, when he wasn't—*she* was the one who was worrying.

He got to the end of the page
and stopped to rest, stretching out
his shoulders. He'd been hunching
forward, peering at the book. Then he
froze. There had been a flash of white
inside the pen. He was sure of it.

Had Daisy moved?

There was no sign of her now—
except for that little wisp of white tail
sticking out.

Slowly, Jack started to read again.
He kept his face down toward the
book, but every so often, he rolled his
eyes sideways to look into the pen.
He was about halfway down the next
page—and how had that happened? It
felt like the fastest he'd ever managed
to read anything—when a black nose
appeared from under the dog bed, and

the stub of tail disappeared. Daisy was wriggling forward. She was listening!

Jack went on. He wasn't sure he'd be able to tell Mr. Gardner what happened on any of those pages, because he was too busy keeping an eye on Daisy, but he *was* reading. And he liked that he was reading about a dog to a dog.

After a few more sentences, the rest of Daisy's muzzle edged out from under the bed, and he could just see her dark eyes glinting at him from under the fabric.

"Oh…," he whispered a couple of minutes

later. "Only one more chapter to go.
Do you like this story?" He peered
at Daisy again and went on talking
quietly. There was more of her sticking
out now. He could see her collar, and
her front paws were showing, too, one
on each side of her nose. Jack flipped
the pages. The last chapter was short,
only a couple of pages. He could do
that. Definitely.

By the time he'd gotten to the end of
the book, Daisy was still lying on the
floor, but only half of her was under
her bed. She lay watching Jack with
her nose on her crossed front paws, and
she really seemed to be listening. As if
she was actually enjoying listening to
him read. Jack couldn't remember the
last time that had happened.

Chapter Five
A Special Visit

Daisy could hear someone talking
outside her pen. It was a quiet voice,
speaking slowly. Some of the people
here had tried to talk to her before—
they'd sat in her pen and tried to coax
her to come out and see them. She
never did. She came out for food and
ate it as fast as she could, but that
was all. Once the lights were off and

the staff had left, she crept out and snuggled on top of her bed. But at the slightest noise—another dog barking or even just shifting in its sleep—she would be right back underneath.

Whoever was talking now hadn't tried to come in to her space. She liked that. They stopped every now and then, the sounds stumbling out. It made the noise seem gentle, and she liked that, too. It was hard to hear, though, underneath her bed.

Very slowly, she edged forward so that her nose stuck out. The boy's reading was clearer now, but then he stopped talking, and she whisked back to the safe darkness under the bed. Slowly, quietly, he started again, and Daisy wriggled out, inch by inch.

Except for the quiet, halting voice, the dog section of the rescue was almost silent. No one was barking. Daisy let her ears flop down, and she rested her muzzle gently on her paws. The fear that had been building up inside her for days eased, just a little, and her eyes half closed as Jack went on.

Jack didn't tell Mattie what had happened—he still wasn't sure he believed it, anyway. It could have been a coincidence that Daisy happened to decide to come out of her hiding place just then. But he really, really hoped not. If he was actually helping, he had to go there again. Mattie wasn't going to be at the rescue for the next couple of days—she had shifts at the supermarket—but she always fit in helping on the weekend. And he was going to go with her.

"Are you sure?" Mattie eyed him sleepily at breakfast on Saturday morning. "You know I'm going

now—before I have to go to work.
As in, you'd better be dressed in three
minutes if you really want to come."

Jack didn't need to think about it.
He dashed upstairs and threw on some
clothes. He was back in the kitchen
before Mattie had gotten halfway
through her cereal.

"Is that okay, Mattie?" Mom asked,
stirring her tea. "Jack won't be in your
way?"

"I'm helpful!" Jack pointed out,
feeling annoyed. "I put the food out
for the dogs, and on Wednesday...."
He trailed off. He'd forgotten he wasn't
going to tell anyone about Daisy.

"On Wednesday what?" Mom asked.

"On Wednesday, I did my homework
at the rescue, and I finished my book,"

Jack went on hurriedly.

"Oh, Jack, that's wonderful!" His mom shook her head. "Why didn't you tell me?"

"I've got another one." Jack sighed. "It's a nonfiction book about sharks. But it looks okay, I guess."

He stuck the book in the pocket of his coat when he set off with Mattie. He wanted to see if Daisy would listen to him reading again. If she came out from under the basket today, it would be like a scientific experiment, where you did the same thing again to make sure you got the same results twice.

He'd been a little worried that there would be a lot of visitors looking at the dogs because it was a weekend— he didn't want a bunch of strangers hearing him read. But when he asked, Mattie explained that they tried to encourage people to look at the dogs online first.

"It's upsetting for the dogs sometimes, having a lot of people walking up and down and pointing at them," she told him as they hung up their coats. "If they look at the dogs online, we can bring the ones they want to meet to the visitors' room, so they can get to know them."

Susan and Adrian and Mattie were busy showing dogs and cats to people hoping to adopt, and whenever they had a spare minute, they were figuring out a plan for a fundraising event at the shopping center close to Jack's school. So no one noticed that

when Jack had finished washing out
the dogs' water bowls, he hurried to
Daisy's pen. Her tail was sticking out
again, but he was sure the lump under
the dog bed looked bigger. She
was growing.

"I've got a new book,"
he explained, waving
it at the wire front
of the pen. "You
probably don't know
what sharks are, but
they're interesting.
They've been around for
hundreds of millions of years—I never
knew that until I got this book."

He settled down next to the pen and
opened up the page about great whites.
He started to read, glancing sideways

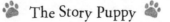

hopefully every so often to see if Daisy was listening.

It took a little while, but by the time Jack was reading about shark attacks— there were only between five and ten attacks on humans every year, which he was surprised about—Daisy had poked her head out from under the bed to listen. When he had read the last of the photo captions on that page, Jack risked looking over at her.

"Hey…," he whispered. The puppy was peering at him, with her nose resting on her paws. When he spoke to her, he was sure he saw the dog bed bounce a little. Was she actually wagging her tail? He didn't want to scare her, so he quickly went back to reading out loud.

When Jack got to the end of the page, Daisy was sitting by the wire, watching him.

"Are you sure?" Amarah asked, looking up at Jack as he leaned over the fence between their yards.

"Ummm. I think I'm sure. She didn't come out for Mattie or any of the staff at the rescue. I think she likes being read to. We're going over to the rescue in a minute, so do you want to come and see if she'll do it for you, too? Mattie won't mind and Susan will be okay with it if we bring a note from your mom. We can help Mattie wash bowls or do something else useful first."

Amarah nodded. "I'll go and see if it's okay." She raced off and was back in a couple of minutes. "She said yes! Should I climb over the fence?" Both yards had benches in just the right place to make it easy to do. "Mom! I'm going now!" She hopped up onto the back of the bench and swung one leg over.

"I'll tell Mattie." Jack dashed into the house.

"Amarah wants to come, too?" Mattie stared at him in surprise when he explained. "Why?"

"Because I told her all about Daisy, and she wants to see her. We'll both help."

"Um, okay. But you have to be careful," Mattie said, smiling at Amarah as she came in through the back door. "Daisy's so shy, Amarah. We can't scare her. Though actually I noticed she was a little braver yesterday when I brought her dinner in. She looked at me! I know that doesn't sound like much, but it is."

Jack exchanged a hopeful glance with Amarah. It really sounded as if his reading was making Daisy feel better.

At the rescue, Susan let them help groom two long-haired cats, and play with the black-and-white kittens that Jack had seen before. After that, though, they managed to hurry to Daisy's pen before someone could give them another job to do.

The puppy was curled up on her side, but only half tucked under her bed this time—as though she wanted to be close enough to dart back underneath, just in case. She watched cautiously as Jack and Amarah approached her. Then instead of hiding, she wriggled up onto her paws and came to stand by the wire.

"She never did that before!" Jack whispered.

"You'd better read to her," Amarah breathed. "She almost looks like she's waiting for you to start."

Jack sat on the floor and started to read the page in his book about sawfish. A couple of sentences in, Daisy sat down by the wire front of the pen and yawned.

"She definitely likes it," Amarah whispered, and Jack nodded to her. It was almost relaxing, reading with Daisy listening. He'd been worried that Amarah being there would make him feel awkward, but Amarah was more interested in the dogs than she was in him. When he got to the end of the page, she waved a hand at him.

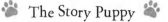

"The others are listening, too. Did you know?"

Jack glanced around at the rest of the pens. The dogs *were* all very quiet. Even Pug, who had the pen two down from Daisy, wasn't barking and whining the way he usually did. Jack held the book out to Amarah. "Here," he whispered. "You try. Read some of it to Pug— usually he's yapping all the time."

"Okay...." Amarah took the book and sat down in front of Pug's pen. Jack could hear him panting as he came to the wire front to see what was going on. Then he started to bark. Amarah looked anxiously at Jack.

"Am I making him upset?"

"No, he barks a lot, honestly. Read to him. Let's see."

Amarah started reading, talking nervously over Pug's barks at first, but then slowing down as she began to relax. Pug seemed to relax, too. He stopped yapping, and then he slumped down to the floor of the pen and started to chew on a rubber bone as he listened.

"It really does work," Jack said, looking around. Pug was chewing. Daisy had gone to lie down, but on top of her bed this time. Bandit, the big collie mix, was slumped on the floor of his pen, looking half asleep.

Amarah nodded. "They love it."

81

Chapter Six
Getting Better

"She's gotten so much better."

Jack nodded, looking down proudly at Daisy. The little white puppy was standing on her hind legs, sniffing Susan's fingers. It had been two weeks since Jack had first seen her, and Daisy hardly ever hid under her basket now—only when there was a lot of barking from the other dogs.

Susan had let him go into the pen with Daisy a few times—after they'd checked with Mom— and it was a real treat, getting to pet her and give her attention. Her white fur looked as if it would be wiry, but she was incredibly soft, and her peachy ears were like warm velvet. Jack couldn't help imagining sitting on the couch at home with her, rubbing those ears while they watched TV.

"You wouldn't think she was the same dog," Mattie said, crouching down to let Daisy sniff her hands, too, and Daisy wagged her tail wildly.

"She still has a long way to go, but she's getting really friendly." Susan smiled at Jack. "Who knew reading to a dog could make such a difference!"

Jack beamed back at her. Since he'd discovered the secret—it still felt like a secret, an amazing discovery—he had been going back to the rescue with Mattie as often as he could. He could visit for a short time after school most weekdays, and he got to be there for longer on the weekends. Since it was a Sunday, he'd been helping Susan all afternoon, and she'd let him take some of the dogs into the little yard so he could throw toys for them to chase. It seemed like a lot of fun to Jack, but

Susan promised it was really useful.

Jack did most of his reading with Daisy, but sometimes he read to the other dogs, too. Pug was definitely less yappy after Jack had sat with him for a while—and it was helping Jack's reading, too. Mr. Gardner had told Mom that there had been *a definite improvement.*

Jack had even been doing extra reading online, trying to find out more ways to help Daisy. He and Amarah had found a rescue website that showed how to make a special treat mat to keep bored dogs busy. Mattie had let him have the scruffy old fleece with holes that she used to wear at the rescue. Mom had given her a new one for her birthday, and Mattie had been planning

to throw the old one away. He and
Amarah had spent a long time cutting
up strips of fabric—Amarah's mom had
given them one of Anika's polo shirts
that was covered in marker, too.

They'd tied the strips through
the holes in the square of fleece,
so it looked like a fluffy mat. Jack
had finished it the night before and
brought it with him to try out with
Daisy when it was time for her dinner.
If she liked it, he was thinking he
could make some more, maybe one for
every dog at the rescue.

"I'm going to help get your dinner
ready now," he told Daisy after Susan
and Mattie had left. He was kneeling
on the floor outside her pen, so her
nose was on a level with his if she

stood on her back legs. He giggled as she swiped her tongue through the wire and licked him, and he had to wipe dog slobber off his cheek. "Ugh. I love you, too. Back in a bit, okay?"

In the kitchen, Jack helped Mattie measure out the food, and then he took a handful of biscuits from Daisy's bowl and hid them one by one inside the fluffy mat. It was supposed to make eating more fun as the dogs sniffed out the food. *It looks good*, he thought, eyeing it proudly.

"You didn't say you'd finished it!" Mattie said, coming back in to grab more food bowls. "Are you going to try it out?"

"Yeah! Want to come and see?"

They headed back to Daisy's pen,

and Jack put her usual food bowl down first. He had a feeling that if she was really hungry, the treat mat might not be as much fun. If *he* was starving, having to search for his dinner would definitely make him grumpy. Then he left the mat in the corner of the pen, and he and Mattie stood outside to watch.

Daisy wolfed down her food in about a minute, like she usually did, but she could clearly smell that there was more around somewhere. She sniffed her way over to the mat and started to root around in it eagerly, nosing out each biscuit and crunching it up. Jack could tell she really liked it—her tail was wagging excitedly, and her ears were pricked right up.

"That's a hit," Mattie whispered.
"Wow, I thought it would take her
longer. She must have found almost all
the food."

Daisy was slowing down now. She
nibbled one more treat out of the mat
and then slumped down next to it. It
looked as if she was trying to hold the
mat in her paws and cuddle it, and
Mattie put her hand over her mouth to
stop herself from laughing.

"She's going underneath it! Look!"
Jack nudged his sister, and they

watched as Daisy snuffled her way under the treat mat so that she was a little white dog with a fluffy blue head. "I think she's falling asleep. She still likes sleeping with something over her head, doesn't she?"

"Maybe she always will," Mattie said a little sadly. "I suppose dogs remember things they learn when they're little. It's a habit for her now." Then she put her arm around Jack and hugged him. "I'm sorry! I didn't mean to bring you down. She's always going to remember you reading to her, too, you know." Then she looked at her watch and made a face. "I'd better get going with feeding everyone now."

Jack crouched down, watching Daisy breathing gently as she slept. She was still so small that the mat could have covered her completely.

"Hey…," someone whispered next to him.

"Mom!" Jack jumped up. "I didn't even see you."

"I know! I'm sorry. I didn't mean to scare you. Time to head back home."

"Do we have to?" Jack sighed.

"Yes, it's just about your dinner time, too!" Mom smiled at him. "I'm really impressed, you know. You've been spending so much time helping out here."

"I like it. I love dogs—I didn't know how much until I started coming here with Mattie."

Mom nodded. "I can see that." She took a deep breath. "Jack, I've been thinking—would you like us to get a dog of our own?"

Jack stopped watching Daisy's soft, sleepy breathing and turned to stare at his mom. Did she mean it? They could have a dog? They could have Daisy?

He'd never even let himself hope that he could take her home. Earlier on, when Susan had said how much better she was, he'd been so happy. And then a little voice in his head had pointed out, *That means somebody could adopt her soon. Someone's going to take Daisy away. They might even change her name, and she wouldn't be your Daisy anymore.* He'd squashed the voice down, and then Susan had said she still had a long way to go, and the relief had just surged through him. *Not yet!*

"Yes!" he yelped, and Daisy twitched under the treat mat. She wriggled, and then her whiskery muzzle appeared, and her dark eyes shone up at him from under the fluffy fabric. "I mean, yes, that would be amazing," he added in a quieter voice, grinning at Daisy. "She's—"

"I always thought it would be too difficult to cope with, but helping with the dogs here seems to have been so good for you. Of course, we'd have to make sure it was the right dog," Mom went on, and Jack nodded. That made sense. Daisy was absolutely the right dog.

"Probably an older dog who's really calm? I bet Susan could help us choose one."

Jack went on nodding for a second or two until he actually heard what Mom had said. *An older dog. Calm.*

"It wouldn't be good to have a puppy. We don't have time to do a lot of training when we're all so busy. But I could pop home from work at lunchtime to do a quick walk, and maybe Mattie could, too, sometimes."

Jack kept his eyes fixed on Daisy. He'd been so excited, so happy, for all of half a minute. How could only thirty seconds of hoping make everything seem so much worse now? It was as if he'd been given the most amazing present and then had it snatched away from him again. In fact, that was exactly what had happened.

From underneath the raggedy mat, Daisy watched Jack walk away, her ears drooping. He was leaving! He never went without saying good-bye to her. Even if he was on the other side of the wire, he always rubbed her ears and told her how beautiful she was.

She scrambled up, whining, but he didn't turn and run back. It was as if he couldn't even hear her. She whined louder, scratching her claws against the wire door, and then she gave a sharp little bark—but Jack disappeared around the corner of the hallway without even looking back.

She stared out for a moment or two, her nose jammed in the gap between the wires. Then she turned away and picked up the treat mat in her teeth. It smelled like Jack—Jack and biscuits. Daisy took the mat with her as she crawled underneath her bed.

Chapter Seven
A Worrisome Time

"What's the matter with you?" Amarah hissed as Mr. Gardner turned away.

Jack just shrugged.

"You knew how to do that problem! Why didn't you do it?"

"Just leave me alone!" Jack stretched his legs out under the table and kicked Aaron's chair leg. And again. And then again.

"Hey! Stop it!" Aaron muttered. "I can tell it's you, Jack."

"Mr. Gardner's watching you," Lily said in a sing-song voice. "You'll get in trouble!" She sounded very excited about it.

Jack stopped kicking Aaron's chair and wrapped his feet around the legs of his own chair instead. He felt like he needed to glue himself down. It had been the same ever since yesterday. Mom and Mattie kept talking about dogs at the rescue, and which ones would make good pets. They both seemed really excited about it. Mom was even thinking about adopting Pug.

All he wanted to do was yell, *No! It has to be Daisy! I only want Daisy!* How could they even think he'd ever be happy with a different dog?

He made a strange noise, a sort of choking, gasping noise, and Amarah looked at him sharply. "Are you going to be sick?"

Jack shook his head, but he wasn't actually sure. He felt awful.

"Here." Amarah handed him her water bottle, and he gulped from it gratefully. He wasn't going to be sick; it was just that he really, really wanted to cry, he realized. But he couldn't, not here, not in front of everybody.

"Is something wrong with Daisy?" Amarah whispered, and Jack stared at her.

"How did you know?"

Amarah shrugged. "Hunch. You've been so much better at school since you started helping at the rescue and spending all that time with her. Now you've gone back to being weird and moody again."

"Who's Daisy?" Lily leaned over to ask. "Oooooh! Does Jack have a *girlfriend*?"

Amarah scowled at her. "Grow up," she snapped. "What are you, five?" and Lily's face turned scarlet.

Jack put his hand over his mouth to stop himself from laughing out loud. "Thanks," he muttered to Amarah.

"My mom said we could adopt a dog."

Amarah shook her head. "I don't get it! That's fantastic! Why are you upset?" Then she stared down at her math problems like it was the most interesting thing she'd ever seen. "Mr. Gardner's glaring at us," she said out the side of her mouth. "Tell me at recess, okay?"

At recess, Amarah dragged Jack over to one of the benches and handed him half her banana. "I don't understand. I thought you really wanted a dog!"

Jack shook his head gloomily
and squished the end of the banana
between his fingers. He couldn't face
eating it. "Nope. I want Daisy."

"So why can't you adopt her? Is she
still too little? You could wait a while,
though, couldn't you?"

"It isn't that. Mom says we need to
get an older dog who's calm. You know,
well behaved. No puppies, because
they're too hyper."

"What, so your mom doesn't want
a dog version of you?" Amarah gave a
snort.

Jack sighed. "Yeah."

"I'm sorry." Amarah's face fell. "That
was meant to be a joke."

"It's true, though."

"But you've been a lot better,"

Amarah pointed out. "Mr. Gardner
told your mom how good you've been.
I heard him. That's all because of
Daisy. Doesn't your mom understand
that? Why didn't you tell her?"

"I don't know! I didn't think she'd
listen. She said not a puppy." Jack
handed the banana back to Amarah
and wrapped his arms tightly around
his middle, as if he was giving himself
a hug.

"Yes, but Daisy's not just *any* puppy,
is she?" Amarah shook her head. "You
have to tell her. Didn't your sister say
anything? Mattie knows how special
Daisy is."

"Yeah…." Jack leaned back against
the bench. "Maybe Mom would listen
to Mattie," he admitted.

"Mattie, and me, and you," Amarah said firmly. "Your sister's taking you to the rescue again this afternoon, isn't she? So you have to explain everything to her. You can both tell your mom later, and I'll come over and tell her, too."

Jack nodded slowly. Maybe Amarah was right—he *hadn't* told Mom how he felt about Daisy; he'd just expected her to know. He had to speak up.

Daisy's nose was just poking out from under her bed, but she'd pulled the bed up close to the wire door so she could see what was happening. She was watching for Jack. Every time anyone had walked down the hallway that day, she'd wriggled out a little more to see who it was. But it was never him. Daisy knew that usually Jack came later on, but still she couldn't help hoping. She was starting to feel hungry for dinner now, and he often arrived just before dinnertime. Soon....

There was some scuffling, and footsteps, and Daisy scooted out from under the bed to look down the hallway. There was a boy.... Her ears pricked up hopefully.

No, not Jack yet. It was Susan with a group of people Daisy didn't know.

"We do have one adorable young puppy actually, but she's a little nervous. I'm not sure she's ready for a busy family home just yet."

The group moved off toward
the main reception
area, and Daisy
slumped down
on the floor
again. When
was he going
to come?

Then her tail
hunched between her
legs, and a shudder ran over her. What
if he didn't come back? What if he'd
left her, like the people who'd thrown
her out of the car? Daisy was almost
sure that Jack was hers. But they had
been her people, too.

She whimpered and scratched at the
blue treat mat under her paws to catch
the smell of food, and Jack, and home.

Jack ran down the hallway to the
corner where Daisy's pen was. He had a
strange feeling in his stomach, as if she
might have disappeared. All afternoon
he'd been daydreaming—whenever Mr.
Gardner wasn't watching, anyway—
thinking about what would happen
after he'd explained everything to
Mom. He *had* to make her understand.
Amarah was right.

He'd imagined running around
the park with Daisy. Or Daisy asleep
on his lap while he was doing his
homework or watching TV. Maybe
even asleep on the end of his bed. It
all felt so real; it was too good to be
true....

No, there she was, scratching wildly at the side of her pen. She was so excited that she was actually squeaking.

"Did you miss me?" Jack asked her, laughing. He caught her paws through the wire pen, hot little paws with hard black nails. "I missed you. Let me look at you…." It felt as if he was looking at her properly for the first time, now that there was a chance, just a chance, that she might be his dog.

She was so beautiful, even when she was jumping up and down and then darting off to whirl around her pen and flinging herself back to lick frantically at his fingers.

"Shhh, shhh…," Jack said gently. "It's okay, Daisy. It's okay."

There were footsteps at the other

end of the hallway, and he saw Susan
walking toward him with Mattie
behind her. Susan had a clipboard
and a pen—she was tapping the pen
against her teeth as if she was thinking.

"Hello! How's she doing, Jack?"

"Good. She was a little excited, but
she's calming down now." Jack looked
back at Daisy, who was standing close
to the wire, looking uncertain.

"I was just talking to a family who is
looking for a puppy," Susan explained.
"Or a young dog, anyway." She
sighed. "I did try to suggest one of our
beautiful older dogs, but they wanted a
dog who'd be really active. Anyway—"
she smiled at Jack—"I wondered about
Daisy. What do you both think?" She
looked over at Mattie. "You've done so

much work socializing her, especially you, Jack. Do you think she'd be okay with a family? It's actually only one boy and he's ten, so he's not too young."

Mattie nodded eagerly. "I think they'd have to take things slowly, but yes. Daisy's such a beautiful dog; she deserves a loving home."

"No!" Jack yelped, and Daisy gave a worried whine and scraped one front paw against the concrete.

Mattie frowned at him. "Hey, gently."

"I'm sorry." Jack swallowed hard. He had to get this right. He had to make Susan and Mattie understand— he'd meant to talk to Mom first, but he couldn't let Susan give Daisy to somebody else. Not *his* dog. He crouched down and let Daisy snuffle at his fingers while he tried to think of what to say.

"Did Mattie tell you that our mom said we could adopt a dog?" he asked Susan.

She nodded, smiling. "Yes, it's wonderful news. I know Mattie's been desperate to have one for a while, and you're just such a dog person, Jack."

Jack tried to smile back, but his face felt stiff. "Maybe. I'm not sure if I'm really a dog person. It's … I mean … I only want Daisy!"

"Oh…." Mattie started to shake her head. "But Mom said…."

"I know," Jack broke in quickly. "We have to have an older dog." He nodded at Susan. "But Mom's saying that because I'm…." He faltered. "Um. Sometimes I'm not very sensible. Except I am. I could be. If it was Daisy. All that reading to her—I worked really hard—and she's so much better. We're *good* for each other."

Susan beamed at him and reached down to pat his shoulder. "I know you are. You've been amazing with her, and you can tell that she has bonded with you." She glanced at Mattie. "That was actually something I was a little worried about—whether Daisy would ever build up such a good relationship with her new owner. But I couldn't stop Jack from helping her, not when it was making such a difference."

Jack nodded eagerly. "Could you—

please could you tell my mom that? That we don't need an older dog?" He looked hopefully at Mattie. "You like her, too, don't you?"

Mattie crouched down and looked at the little white face peering back at them anxiously through the wire. "Silly question," she said lovingly, and then laughed as Daisy dabbed a cold black nose against her hand. "Okay. Now we just have to convince Mom."

Chapter Eight
A Happy Ending

"I'm not sure about this." Jack's mom sighed. "A puppy! And a puppy who's had a hard time and isn't very reliable! That's exactly what I said I *didn't* want."

Mattie had called her mom and asked her to come by the rescue on her way home from work. Now Mom and Susan and Mattie and Jack were all sitting in the visitors' room with Daisy. Jack had Daisy on his lap, and she was half asleep, curled snugly against his school sweater. It was already covered in white hair, but he didn't mind. He'd get them off with tape if Mom was worried, but he loved that Daisy had left a mark on him. It felt like he belonged to her.

Susan nodded seriously. "I know exactly what you mean. But actually, she's settling down amazingly well. She was very young when we got her, and yes, she'd been abandoned, and she was very withdrawn and nervous, but that's changed over the last few weeks. And I have to tell you, that's mostly because of Jack." She smiled at him, and Jack grinned back at her shyly. He still wasn't used to people saying such nice things about him. "He's worked so hard. He's too young to be an official volunteer at the rescue like Mattie, but I'm really hoping he'll keep coming to help. Even when you have your own dog at home, Jack."

Jack nodded eagerly. "My friend Amarah wants to keep coming here, too," he told Susan. "We wondered—do you think you could make it an official thing, us reading to the dogs? They all like it. And we thought maybe we could send a message to the schools around here, asking for more volunteers. So that there's someone reading to the dogs after school every day. Or some schools might walk children to the rescue during their lunch break."

"Wow." Susan blinked, looking surprised. "We could definitely think about it."

"It would mean more people coming to the rescue," Mattie pointed out. "We're always trying to think of ways to get more people in to see the dogs and cats."

Jack nodded. There were so many dogs who'd been at the rescue for a long time—they were desperate for loving homes. He ran one of Daisy's soft ears through his fingers, and she snuffled sleepily.

"It would help with the children's reading, too," he added. "Schools would like that. I got a lot better just from reading out loud to Daisy and the others."

Susan and Mom were nodding as if they agreed, and Jack ducked his head to hide his proud grin. He was persuading them!

"That all sounds great," Jack's mom said slowly, "but I'm still worried about us adopting Daisy. How are we going to cope with a puppy?"

"It's tricky," Susan admitted. "We usually say that someone needs to be home most of the time to make sure young dogs aren't lonely."

"I can pop home from school if I have a free period," Mattie pointed out. "Most days I do. And you said you could come home at lunchtime, Mom. She'd get a lot of little walks. Jack and I could take her out for a run before school."

"Amarah asked her mom this afternoon," Jack said eagerly. "She said she doesn't mind coming over to check on Daisy sometimes, too. Daisy's so good, Mom; just look at her." He edged closer to his mom on the couch, and the puppy opened one eye lazily and yawned. "Do you want to pet her?" he asked.

Mom reached out one hand and ran it gently down Daisy's back. "She's very soft," she told Jack, smiling. "Hello, sweetheart…," she added as Daisy wriggled around and licked the back of her hand. "You are very cute, aren't you? And I can see how much she loves you both. Maybe it would be all right." Then she gave a surprised laugh as Daisy wobbled upright and stomped

over onto her lap
instead. The little
white dog slumped
down again with
a huge yawn and
seemed to go back
to sleep. "Oh … I
wasn't expecting that."
Mom rubbed Daisy's ears
and looked up at Jack and Mattie.
"I think she might have decided for
us…."

Daisy wriggled a little in Jack's arms,
turning so she could gaze up at him.
He looked afraid, and she could smell
the worry rising off him. She pressed

her nose gently into the gap under his chin and felt him catch his breath in a half laugh. "Thanks," he whispered, rubbing his cheek against the top of her head. "This is really scary."

Daisy felt him step forward, and then Amarah held up a piece of paper in front of her nose. Daisy leaned out of Jack's arms to sniff it, and then she nibbled the bottom corner. The crowd of people in front of them laughed, and Daisy beat her tail against Jack's arm. She didn't know what was happening, but she liked the noise. Jack started to read out loud.

"Thank you for coming to the fundraiser for Tall Pines Animal Rescue. Today we are launching a new program to help animals, and children…."

Daisy sighed happily, resting her nose on his shoulder.

"I started to read to my dog, Daisy, when she was brought to Tall Pines after being abandoned. I didn't know the amazing effect that reading to dogs could have, not only on her, but on me, too. Please help us...."

"You did so well!" Mattie hugged Jack, trying not to squash Daisy, and Daisy squirmed delightedly. "I could hear people in the crowd saying how beautiful Daisy is."

"I can't believe I read in front of all those people," Jack said. He was still feeling a little shaky.

"I can't believe you did, either. You were wonderful." Mattie rubbed Daisy's nose. "And so were you, little one."

"Susan says a lot of people are asking about making appointments to visit," Amarah told them excitedly, pointing at the board behind Jack, which was plastered with big photos of the dogs at the rescue. "Someone wants to come and see Pug! She said she's always had pugs, and he's really beautiful!"

"I'd better go and help write down some details," Mattie said, darting away, and Jack sat down on the edge of the little stage. Daisy wriggled out of his arms and started to sniff around their feet. The shopping center was full of intriguing smells.

"How are you doing?" Amarah asked, sitting next to him. "I was worried that you might run away just before it was time for your speech."

"Me, too." Jack shivered. "But it was okay. It sounded like I was talking to the crowd, but actually I just read it to Daisy."

Daisy heard her name and looked

around. Then she jumped up next to him again, squeezing in between Jack and Amarah and nosing lovingly at both of them. She sank down with her muzzle on Jack's knee and gazed up at him with huge, dark eyes.

"Do you want to go home?" Jack whispered to her. "Me, too. It's okay, Daisy. We'll be home soon, I promise."

Daisy thumped her tail lazily against Amarah's legs and then wriggled farther up so that she was slumped half onto Jack's lap. She didn't mind where they went, as long as Jack came with her.